Joseph Aloysius Lyons

The Malediction

A Drama in Three Acts

Joseph Aloysius Lyons

The Malediction
A Drama in Three Acts

ISBN/EAN: 9783337376819

Printed in Europe, USA, Canada, Australia, Japan

Cover: Foto ©Andreas Hilbeck / pixelio.de

More available books at **www.hansebooks.com**

A Drama

IN THREE ACTS. TRANSLATED FROM THE FRENCH, AND ADAPTED
FOR MALE CHARACTERS ONLY.

WITH STAGE DIRECTIONS, CAST OF CHARACTERS, RELATIVE POSITIONS, ETC.

BY

Joseph A. Lyons, A. M.

———

NOTRE DAME, INDIANA:
UNIVERSITY PRESS.
1883.

DEDICATION.

To the Members of the

ST. CECILIA PHILOMATHEAN SOCIETY,

PAST, PRESENT, AND YET TO BE,

This Drama,

ALREADY FAMILIAR IN THEIR HISTORY,

And Endeared to their Recollections,

IS RESPECTFULLY INSCRIBED

By One

WHOSE BRIGHTEST REMINISCENCES,

For a Quarter of a Century,

ARE OF THE HOURS

Passed in their Society.

J. A. L.

Notre Dame, Indiana,
Dec. 8, 1883.

DRAMATIS PERSONÆ.

Don Vasco de Gomez, a Spanish nobleman.

Don Alonzo, Son of Don Vasco.

Don Lopez, friend of Alonzo.

Tarik, Lieutenant to the Caliph.

Pedro, a Peasant.

Pedrillo,   } Sons of Pedro.
Fabricio,   }

Ibrahim, a rich Mahometan.

Mendoza, Spanish Officer.

Marietto,
Basilio,
Sancho,   } Spanish Soldiers.
Virgilio,

Juanino, Slave of Ibrahim.

Abdallah, Mahometan Jailer.

Jirmibechlich, a Turkish Slave.

Spanish Soldiers, Mahometan Soldiers, Peasants,
etc.

In the second act, Alonzo is called Almanzor, and in the third, Fernando. In the second act, Lopez is called Soliman.

COSTUMES.

Don Vasco. A rich brown Spanish dress, trimmed with gold lace, slashed with black satin, silk stockings, with gold clocks, black shoes, large Spanish hat with black feathers, one red ditto, point lace collar and cuffs.

Don Alonzo.—*First Dress:* Rich emerald green velvet Spanish dress, slashed with white satin, jacket of white satin, cloak of white satin, turn back, embroidered with broad philacteries of dead and bright gold, white hat, white feathers, white silk stockings, shoes with gold and satin rosettes, and dress trimmed with satin of the same. *Second Dress:* Scarlet turban, scarlet mantle, white sarsnet robe, and cestus richly ornamented, copper-colored pantaloons and red sandals. *Third Dress:* Old blue velvet trunks, leather doublet, brown velvet sleeves, old brown sombrero, torn lace collar, old silk stockings.

Don Lopez.—Amber jacket, purple velvet cloak, trunks richly trimmed with gold, and bows of crimson satin ribbon, drab hat with one feather, russet boots, point lace cuffs and collar. *Second Dress:* Like Don Alonzo, but in green colors.

Tarik.—Handsome Turkish fly of scarlet and gold, amber shirt of merino reaching below the knee, white merino Turkish trowsers, russet boots, scimitar, scarlet turban with gold crescent.

Ibrahim. — White Moorish dress with deep broad purple stripe. Green turban.

Pedro. — Blue shirt trimmed with orange, with heavy hanging sleeves, and bonnet with single plume.

Pedrillo and Fabricio.—The same, in colors green and pink, respectively.

Mendoza.—Black silver jacket and trunks, puffed with yellow satin and gold, scarlet silk tights, russet boots, red rosettes, gauntlets, Spanish hat, white plumes, lace collar, sword, etc.

Spanish Soldiers. — Buff coats and full Spanish breeches, buff boots, helmets and breastplates.

Juanino. Plain shirt with red leggings.

Abdallah. Red Turkish fly, breastplate underneath, plain white shirt, Turkish pantaloons, russet boots, white turban, scimitar.

Jirmibechlich.—Blue Turkish fly, white shirt reaching below the knee, blue Turkish trowsers.

Mahometan Soldiers. Scarlet Turkish fly, moderately trimmed with silver and gold, breastplates underneath, white shirts, Turkish pantaloons, russet boots, scarlet turbans, scimitars.

Peasants.—Same as Pedro, but in various colors.

EXITS AND ENTRANCES.

R. means *Right;* L. *Left;* R. D. *Right Door;* L. D. *Left Door;* S. E. *Second Entrance;* U. E. *Upper Entrance;* M. D. *Middle Door.*

RELATIVE POSITIONS.

R. means *Right;* L. *Left;* C. *Centre;* R. C. *Right of Centre;* L. C. *Left of Centre.*

PREFACE.

THE plot of this play is laid in Spain, during the Mahometan wars. Don Alonzo, son of Don Vasco de Gomez, a princely nobleman, is persuaded by ambition and the evil counsel of his confidant, Don Lopez, to abandon his father, his country, and his God. He becomes a prince among the Mahometans, and, in the progress of the war, his father and all his soldiers fall into the hands of Tarik, the Mahometan commander. Tarik commands Don Alonzo to visit his father, and endeavor to win him to the faith of the Prophet, assuring him that if he fails, his father shall die. Alonzo obeys; his father, with righteous indignation, repels him, and pronounces upon him a terrible malediction, beneath which he withers and loses his reason.

Don Vasco and his vassals escape from the Turks and return to the Christian camp, where they find Don Alonzo, who, under his father's care, returns to reason, and is afterwards killed in a battle with the Mahometans. Pedrillo, the peasant, is a man of many words but few actions. He excites a great deal of merriment, and in the last scene shows his skill as a swordsman by killing Tarik in a scientific manner. The play abounds in thrilling incidents. The situations are natural, the diction is forcible, and in all particulars it is an excellent and highly meritorious play.

THE MALEDICTION.

————o————

A DRAMA IN THREE ACTS.

————

ACT FIRST.

SCENE I.

A view of the Asturias. On the right is the postern of the castle of
DON VASCO; MENDOZA, MARIETTO, BASILIO, discovered; SANCHO on
duty at the postern. Groups of Soldiers: some playing dice, others
grouped about MENDOZA.

MARIETTO. Five, eight, fourteen.

BASILIO. Pair of fives, won!

MARIETTO. To the dogs with the game! I'll play no
more.

BASILIO. Hold, Marietto; come, take your revenge.

MARIETTO. Done! I take the moustaches of the first Mahometan who falls beneath my sword.

VIRGILIO (*Singing*):

> And sell not the skin of bear
> Until you've slept in open air.

MARIETTO. May the wig of Mahomet make a turban for
me if I don't cut off enough of their beards to make half a
dozen cushions for myself.

BASILIO. Well said! And when will the affair take
place?

VIRGILIO. As soon as King Pelagius gives orders for us
to pommel the shoulders of these infidels.

MARIETTO. For my part, I'd like to make a mess of the ears and noses of my prisoners. (*To* MENDOZA.) What say you, Mendoza?

BASILIO. Oh! he's probably thinking of some new hymn of glory. Come, Mendoza, a few couplets; they'll aid us to pass away the time.

MARIETTO. That beautiful romance, you know, that awakens such enthusiasm.

MENDOZA. Most willingly, brave comrades. God and the king are the most worthy subjects of our songs:

> As if by some satanic spell
>   Mahomet's hordes possess the land;
> At his approach our cities fell;
>   The prophet false speaks to command.
> Noble race of gallant Spain,
>   Like mine your hearts repeat the ring;
> Freedom for our land maintain,
>   All for our country and our king.
>
> 'Midst a heap of ruins piled
>   My mother died beneath their trod;
> Looked on their bloody hands and smiled,
>   And begged for mercy as from God.
> Too weak and feeble were my hands
>   To then avenge her cruel death;
> But when in ire my heart expands,
>   It breathes but vengeance every breath.
>
> Then take thy bound, my gallant steed,
>   In glorious fields of old Castile;
> From home and friends I soon must speed,
>   The foeman's heart must take my steel.
> 'Tis wish of God and fatherland,
>   The martial war-song we will sing;
> The clarion's note calls all to stand
>   And fight for God and for our king.

[*Enter* DON VASCO. R. 2 E.]

DON VASCO. Well done, brave soldiers! The good cause you have espoused does not allow one thought of sorrow. If at any time, when beholding our beautiful country covered with ruins, your angry passions are aroused, remember that God has ordained us to avenge her wrongs. Brave companions of Pelagius, re-enter your fort and rest yourselves from the fatigues of the night; I myself will keep guard for you. (*Exeunt soldiers* L E.) (*To* BASILIO.) Basilio!

BASILIO. My Lord!

Don V. Come here, my brave fellow! You are gifted with great courage and address, and therefore I confide to you a mission which will demand your greatest prudence and coolness of judgment, with a firm devotion to our cause in every danger. May I rely upon you?

BASILIO. You may, my Lord.

Don V. Good! You are without doubt aware that Pelagius, saluted King of Spain by a band of faithful subjects, is about to raise aloft the national standard in the mountains of Asturia. He calls to himself all those who upon this good old soil have preserved their faith, and the desire of independence which it continually awakens. Castile, Aragon, the mountains of Navarre and Biscay have responded to the call of their respected king; Spain too will soon rise as a single man, and range her hosts under his dauntless colors. Go, then, my brave comrade: outwit the enemies who surround us; find King Pelagius and tell him that, here, our hearts and arms are his. Tell him that Vasco de Gomez has never bowed to the haughty banner of Mahomet; that the flag of Spain still floats in triumph from the ramparts of his castle, and the faith of the soldier of Christ still burns strongly within his devoted bosom.

BASILIO. I go, my Lord, and if I succeed not in fulfilling your commands, 'twill be that death has claimed me before I could avenge my country's wrongs.

Don V. Farewell, Basilio. May God and our Lady of Sorrows guard you. (*Exeunt in opposite directions.*)

SCENE II.

[*The same.* SANCHO *on guard.* PEDRILLO *enters*, R. 3 E., *singing.*]

SANCHO. Who goes there?

PEDRILLO. Who goes there! Why, myself, to be sure; at least, I think so.

SANCHO (*angrily*). Who goes there? Quick: speak!

PEDRILLO. Confound you! Must I speak a dozen times! It is I, as I told you! I, Pedrillo, son of Pedro, tenant of Lord Vasco, who's known all round the world! D'ye know me now? But am I awake? Can I believe my eyes? No! —Yes,—but—but is—th—at you, Sancho?

SANCHO. Well yes; I'm Sancho, made into a soldier.

PEDRILLO. I thought something must have happened when you couldn't recognize an acquaintance. But what are you doing there?

SANCHO. What am I doing? Why, you blockhead, don't you see I'm on guard!

PEDRILLO. And who told you to stop me?

SANCHO. Well, you see, I took you for a Mahometan.

PEDRILLO. The devil! do I look like one!

> Think you it's I would follow Mahomet?
> Since when have I passed for a fool?
> Of folly you must have come to the summit,
> Or stand much in need of a little more school.
> He comes out and boldly forbids us to drink;
> Who ever heard of aught of the kind?
> It must be the devil that taught him to think,
> Or else he has fairly gone out of his mind.

I say, Sancho, you treat this subject too lightly; so, to prove what I sang, here's a little flask of old Pedro's choicest (*shows an enormous bottle*); and, if you wish to try it, it is at your service.

SANCHO. Of course, I'll take a drop!

PEDRILLO. At the same time, I'll dine on a little crust I've got here. Come, sit down (*they sit*); take a drink. (*Sancho drinks.*) My turn now (*Pedrillo drinks. Both drink many times*).

SANCHO. (*Wiping his mouth.*) Now, Pedrillo, what brought you here this morning?

PEDRILLO. (*Eating and drinking.*) What brought me here! Well, I don't know much about it; but I'll tell you all I do know (*drinks*). You must remember that it was in the village of Santiago I first saw the light of day. (*Drinks.*) This village, as you know, is just on the boundaries of the province of Don Pelagius. For two days I was at home, thinking of nothing—of nothing more than usual—when, all at once, I heard a noise that made my blood run cold from my feet to my head. Not that I got scared,—but (*rising quickly*) Sancho, Sancho!—di—di—did—n't you hear a—a—a noise?

SANCHO. No, nothing; go on.

PEDRILLO. Hold, till I take a drink (*drinks*). This was a most unearthly cry; then followed groans,—then an uproar; and, slap! bang! down came the blood-thirsty Mahometans to take possession of our village, and each one looked as if he'd like to make a stew of all the noses, ears, and heads in the place.

SANCHO.   Indeed!

PEDRILLO.   Having more than a slight regard for the preservation of my ears and head, I thought the most proper thing to do would be to avoid these ignorant barbarians; and not caring for danger, for I am never afraid, I jumped through the window and started across the fields, when two of the brutes jumped and, striking me with the flat of their sabres, ordered me to march on before them.   I obeyed.   I always obey. And when we reached their camp, where they needed several fine men, I was placed aside as one of the most distinguished. The lieutenant of the caliph looked at me and was much pleased with my features.   "Dog!" said he.   You know, Sancho, when these strange men say "dog" they mean the same as when we say "dear friend."   "Dog! you come from the village of Santiago?"   "That I do," replied I, with a grand bow; just like this, d'ye see (*bows like a Turk*).   "Hold, dog!" he continued, most friendly; "take this letter to Don Alonzo de Gomez.   One hundred pieces of gold if you bring me an answer; five hundred lashes if you fail and ever again fall into our hands."   He gave the letter; I brought it; now I wait for some one to open the gates that I may give it to Alonzo in person.

SANCHO.   (*Rising quickly.*)   You'll not have long to wait; for, hark! he is just coming.

[*Enter* ALONZO *and* LOPEZ.   R. 1 E.]

LOPEZ.   Why do you hesitate, my Lord? circumstances were never more favorable.   Spain, well nigh crushed by the Mahometans, has little hope of rising from her ruined state.   Tarik, all-powerful, offers thrones to those of noble birth who discard their harrassed religion; the discouraged people have given an example of apostasy; the approaching ruin of your house, the hatred you bear to Pelagius—all urge you to follow the multitude and win its foolish love of novelty.   Tarik proposes an alliance with you; he offers you gold, dignities, honors!   Accept them, Alonzo; accept.

ALONZO.   And my God, my father, and my king?

LOPEZ. Your father, overcome by his old prejudices, abhors the Crescent; he believes that the position for every true Spaniard is beneath the standard of the Cross! Leave him to his ideas, but do not allow them to enter your heart; leave him to his belief, it makes him happy; but we want it not. Your king! Has Pelagius, chosen by a few powerful chieftains, a right to this title? Is it right that the blood of Rodrigo should take possession of the throne? Are you not of nobler birth and lineage than he? A hundred others, braver than Pelagius, may dispute his power! And what power! A few square leagues of sterile mountains, a handful of ragged soldiers, and a horde of ambitious chiefs; a power which extends no farther than the territory occupied by the feet of his soldiers. Your God! Alonzo, does He restrain you when, in your nightly orgies—when, in the depth of your debaucheries, you defy His power. Think you of Him when you pour out gold to gratify the cravings of your passions; or, thought you of Him when, in Granada, you pillaged the venerated sanctuaries of the Christians and destroyed their sacred vessels and precious reliquaries? For you and me, the God of the Christians and the God of Mahomet are the same. Gold, power, and honors are the divinities that merit our homage.

ALONZO. Have you finished, Lopez?

LOPEZ. I have.

ALONZO. And think you, you have seduced me by your subtle sophisms? Deny my father! Abjure my God! Yes, *my God!* for do you not see, Lopez, that I still perceive how numerous are my crimes; what numberless profanations I have committed; and that, with sorrow, deep and sincere, I now confess them. I feel there is a God—the good and righteous God of the Christian! You will call this a prejudice, shameful and childish; we can't help it. God indeed exists; and when I reflect within myself, and search into the innermost depths of my heart, all force of reason disappears before this prejudice, and I am left feeble as a child. Renounce my God! would you do it, Lopez?

LOPEZ. My Lord, if I had a terrible injury to avenge; if, like you, I had been repulsed by Pelagius; if, like you, I had heretofore made a profession of atheism, I would not hesitate.

ALONZO. You have not answered.

PEDRILLO. (*Advancing.*) Don Alonzo!

ALONZO. What do you wish? Speak!

PEDRILLO. 'Pon my word, this is strange; when I have to speak to a nobleman I don't know what to say.

ALONZO. Well, what is it?

PEDRILLO. Yes, my Lord! (*aside*) but then it isn't hard; I have only to say as I was directed: " Your Highness, here is a letter to which I await the reply." It's very simple.

ALONZO. Do you know my patience is not lasting?

PEDRILLO. Ah, well! (*scratching his head*) at present I know very little of what I've got to say. Very well! I am (*saluting*) —My Lord —that is, I come—no! but I've got a letter. (*Searching his pockets, boots, etc., and lastly his hat, where, after much buffoonery, he finds the letter.*) Ah! here it is. (*Salutes again.*) My Lord, a letter that Tarif——

ALONZO. (*With surprise.*) Tarik!

PEDRILLO. Yes, my Lord, that the great Tarif, the lieutenant of the armies of the caliph, the chief of the Mahometans, in a word,—(*aside in a low voice,*) without reckoning that these Mahometans are infamous cut-throats, and have slapped me with the flat of their sabres, and have made me sore from the top of my back-bone to——

ALONZO. And this letter, this letter; for whom is it?

PEDRILLO. For you, my Lord.

ALONZO. Give it to me then, you senseless babbler. (*Snatches the letter.*)

PEDRILLO. (*Aside.*) Look there! the thanks I always get. Senseless! It seems there's nothing else to call a man. Senseless! Well, well! (*Sighs comically.*)

ALONZO. (*To* PEDRILLO.) You may go. (*To guard.*) Stand aside!

PEDRILLO. But——

ALONZO. Begone, I tell you!

PEDRILLO. (*Going out.*) Almost killed with Mahometan sabres; insulted for fulfilling my commission; five hundred lashes in expectation; that is what is called awfully lucky, is it! (*Exit.* L. I E.)

ALONZO. (*Giving open letter to* LOPEZ.) Read, Lopez!

LOPEZ. (*Reading.*)

"LORD ALONZO :—The caliph, our sovereign and sublime lord, whose glances are as the scintillations of the carbuncle, whose mouth exhales perfume sweeter than that of the two Arabias, whose words are as the purest honey, and who sits upon a throne of diamonds, who rules over the mightiest kings and treads under his feet the emperors of the East; conqueror of Christians, successor of Mahomet,— the caliph, I say, has condescended to bestow upon you one of those glances which brings joy to princes and happiness to the people. Knowing well your legitimate resentment against Pelagius, the enemy of the prophet and the contemner of his law, he deigns to honor you with his esteem; he calls you to himself, and proposes, if you correspond with his wishes, to open to you the inestimable treasure of his favors. You can with him possess riches, reputation, and honor. Reflect! On the one hand, slavery or death; on the other, all the happiness that the heart can desire! Be wily and prudent as the serpent, and let your reply reach me as quickly as the gazelle bounds over the desert's burning sand. Allah, God, alone is great, and Mahomet is his prophet.

"TARIK."

You see what he offers you, my Lord; riches, reputation honors. Can you hesitate any longer?

ALONZO. And vengeance, too! The die is cast! Come, Lopez, come; share my good fortune; aid me with your counsels, and sustain me with your reasoning. The Mahometan out posts are not far distant; let us join them at once. Come on! (*They go towards the side.*)

[*Enter* DON VASCO, R. I E.]

DON V. Whither do you go, my son? I have come to seek you. Come here. Why do you appear to avoid me? Is your father's presence hateful to you? Listen to me: I have just now sent word to Pelagius to offer him our services; he relies upon us.

ALONZO. Pelagius relies on me!

DON V. And why not? Has he not rescued the standard of Spain from the opprobrium into which it was cast? Have not all the Christians, true Spaniards, and all our noble old cavaliers gathered 'neath its glorious folds? And what motives——

LOPEZ. But, my Lord, you know—

DON V. Silence, Lopez! Yes, I know that your perfidious counsels are hastening my son to ruin; I know the power you exercise over him; I know your depraved morals, your corrupt maxims, and I should fear—yes, fear—for the welfare of my son, if he came not from the illustrious house of De Gomez. Whatever may be his errors, he will never forget that the noble blood of heavenly saints and of the kings of Spain still courses through his veins. Yes, my son, we are going to unite our vassals and join Pelagius; we leave tomorrow, at break of day.

ALONZO. No, father; I will not set out. Pelagius will never behold me following in his train. Sprung as though he be from royal blood, I owe him nothing. Some of our lords, imposed upon by a vain display of valor, have chosen him as their chief: let them follow him: let them revel in the honors of his palace whose halls are sombre caverns, wherein the richest tapestries are formed of honeyed moss; let them command a miserable band of hireling peasants; let them quench their thirst in the waters of the wayside fountains, and regale themselves with the oaten bread of poverty-stricken mountaineers. Pelagius! I hate him too much ever to serve him!

DON V. And should your hate rule, my son, when there is question of your country? Is this a time to engage in vain disputation? An insolent stranger tramples down our harvests, pillages our cities, burns our cottages, destroys our palaces; his armies mark their progress with heaps of ruins and blood-empurpled soil—and you hesitate. Alonzo, you hesitate! You prefer the gilded halls of shame to the obscure caverns of true honor; you choose slavery rather than liberty,—and you bear the name of Gomez!

ALONZO. Father!

DON VASCO. If you resist the call of your country, can you be true to your God? Ascend your highest towers: look, and everywhere around you behold the infidel crescent replacing the symbol of salvation. Then, beholding our religion humiliated, profaned, and trampled to the dust, can your heart remain untouched! Alonzo, are you a Christian?

ALONZO. Father!——

DON V. Are you a Christian? You hesitate, unhappy wretch! Are you a Christian, I ask you?

ALONZO. (*Lowering his head and speaking with hesitation.*) Yes, father.

DON V. To-morrow, then, at one o'clock, don your

brightest armor, mount your charger, and to-morrow night
will find us in the camp of Pelagius.   Be ready then!
(*Exit*, R. 2 E.)

LOPEZ.   Alonzo.

ALONZO.   Leave me, Lopez; I will not hear you—I am
going with my father.   Yes, father, you have won!   It is
not for you, Pelagius—it is not for you!   It is for honor and
religion!   'Tis my duty conducts me beneath your banners.
Lopez, farewell! farewell!

LOPEZ.   And is it thus, my Lord, that you leave?

ALONZO.   Your counsels have failed to ruin me.   Farewell!

LOPEZ.   Oh! it is ever thus with the great!   We, their
feeble slaves, are kept with care while we serve their evil in-
clinations; but, as a vile instrument, are destroyed and cast
aside when we are no longer useful.

ALONZO.   Lopez! Lopez! you do me wrong—I will
always be your protector.   But why will you not follow me
to the camp of Pelagius?   Are you not, too, a Spaniard and
a Christian?

LOPEZ.   No, my Lord; if Don Alonzo forgets his motives
of hatred, throws aside the fortune that is offered him, and
the means of vengeance so fairly within his grasp, and
slavishly follows Pelagius, Lopez will never do so, my Lord!

ALONZO.   Leave me, I tell you!   My heart, like the
angry sea, is stirred to its lowest depths; and like wild inter-
mingling of the foamy breakers, my mind is confused, my
thoughts confounded.

PEDRILLO.   Five hundred lashes!   Only think of it!
think of it!   There's little fun in it except for that Mahometan!   Nevertheless, if I dared—

ALONZO.   Have you considered, Lopez, that your country
is in danger; that the worship of God has been turned into
mockery?

LOPEZ.   I consider nothing but your weakness and irresolution.

PEDRILLO.   Bah! Lord Alonzo won't eat me, any way!
But, at any rate, I'd be rid of the trouble by speaking to
him (*advances stealthily*).

ALONZO.   My irresolution - my weakness,—Lopez!

PEDRILLO. (*In a subdued tone.*) My Lord!

LOPEZ. Yes, my Lord; your irresolution and feebleness! another would, perhaps, give them more disgraceful names.

ALONZO. Lopez!

LOPEZ. Pardon, my Lord, but I cannot tarry. Go; partake of the phantasies and enthusiasm of a weak old man, while I set out to Tarik. I shall not bring with me the support of a noble name, but in its place my life and the assistance of my arms. What is my country to me? My country lies wherever I may be.

PEDRILLO. (*Louder.*) My Lord!

ALONZO. If it were not for Pelagius—

PEDRILLO. (*Louder.*) My Lord!

ALONZO. (*Quickly.*) Fool! what do you wish now?

PEDRILLO. Is it possible! Again! For a long time I've been called nothing but fool! Pedrillo and fool, I think, must mean about the same! But I don't care.

ALONZO. Well?

PEDRILLO. Well, then, I'd sooner you'd say, "Hold, Pedrillo, you are a fool," than receive five hundred lashes; and, if one might judge by the blows of a sabre, they'll make a fellow jump. That's what I've got to say!

ALONZO. Babbler, you'll make me lose my patience!

PEDRILLO. Babbler—that is to say, my Lord, that I like to profit by the gifts of nature, and that she having given me a tongue, I believe in using it at every opportunity. Gently, gently, my Lord; don't get angry; you see I came for your answer to Lord——O—Lord—Nariff, Cariff, Ratiff.—I don't remember that queer name.

ALONZO. An answer to Tarik (*reflecting*).

PEDRILLO. Yes, my Lord, if it was simply not longer than that 'twould be the same to me, only I'll get five hundred lashes across the back if I don't bring it; and that, you see, is something, not minding that he said to me "Dog,"——

ALONZO. Lopez, tell me what shall I do? What answer shall I make?

LOPEZ. Why ask me, my Lord? my counsels have failed to ruin you.

PEDRILLO. Without minding that he said to me "Dog,"

because you see, my Lord, when he speaks to his friends——

ALONZO. Begone! and await my orders. (*To Lopez.*)
Lopez, you are cruel!

LOPEZ. To-morrow night you will be with Pelagius.

ALONZO. With Pelagius! I know not what demon in-
spires you! Must that execrable name ring forever in my
ears?

LOPEZ. Is not your resolution taken? And what a triumph for your enemy! He will have conquered; you will
have bowed before him. Go, my Lord Alonzo, go! Rejoin him whom, unworthy, you have helped to raise to the
throne; follow in his suite, and increase the number of his
cringing courtiers.

ALONZO. Peace! You but add fire to my anger. You increase my rage! You wish to crush me! You seek nothing
but my ruin! Lopez! Lopez! what can you mean? Alonzo
de Gomez wear the turban, and, beneath the crescent,
combat the people to whom he was called to give laws!

LOPEZ. Farewell, my Lord; I leave you.

ALONZO. Lopez! Lopez! you have triumphed! I will
go with you—I will bear arms against my country and my
father. Are you satisfied? (*Aside.*) Against my God!
(*Aloud.*) Lopez, call that man! (PEDRILLO *enters.*) Peasant,
remain here for an instant and I will be with you. (*To Lopez*). Come, Lopez, I wish you to dictate a reply; sustain
my courage, and assist me to consummate my crime. (*Exeunt*, L. 2 E.)

PEDRILLO. Well, good heavens! what a sorrowful air
Don Alonzo wears! Who knows? perhaps that's the way he
has of showing his good humor. But characters can't change
themselves that way at pleasure; they're not like other things.
I wish he'd give me an answer; because, know you that—
that is—well, it would be terrible bad luck if I'd fall
into the hands of those Mahometans, and then have
them say to me, in a friendly way, "Dog, stand there and let
us take the measure of your back five hundred times with the
lash of our whip." Oh! I fancy it all so well that I can
now perceive all the bushes and trees on the way transformed
into the bearded Mahometans to take part in the farce.

(LOPEZ *and* ALONZO *enter*, L. 2 E., *and cross the stage.*)

LOPEZ. Yes, my Lord, it is better that we should flee this instant; the deepening shades will shroud us, and in a few hours we shall safely reach the camp of Tarik. (*Exeunt,* R. 2 E.)

PEDRILLO. Ha, ha! there they go, without speaking to me; and, clearing off, intend to leave me here. Eh? and, as I live, they take the path that leads to the Mahometans; they argue with the sentinel who opposes them——O God! Lopez has struck him with a poignard! Where shall I run! Help! Murder! Help! (*Enter* DON VASCO *and* MENDOZA, L. 2 E., *with soldiers, in disorder.*)

DON V. What has happened? What means this alarm?

PEDRILLO. Help! Help! Lopez—Sancho—the Mahometans—five hundred blows with the flat of a sabre—look, look! (*Points after* LOPEZ. *Exit* MENDOZA, R. 2 E.)

DON V. Where? What?

PEDRILLO. O! don't touch me! (*Runs in terror to other side of stage.*) I didn't do it,—I assure you I didn't!

DON V. Explain yourself; have you lost your head?

PEDRILLO. My head? No, it's here yet; I haven't lost it. What do you want to do with my head, sir?

DON V. The man is a fool. Soldiers, seize him.

PEDRILLO. (*On his knees*) I beg of you! I beseech you do not kill me, and I will never do it again. (*Enter* MENDOZA, R. 1 E.)

MENDOZA. My God! My Lord! Sancho lies murdered below, bathed in his blood. The stiletto buried in his breast bears the name of Lopez.

DON V. O God! Where is my son? To arms! brave comrades, to arms! Mendoza, our swiftest horses! quick! To arms! To arms!

END OF THE FIRST ACT.

ACT SECOND.

SCENE I.

Interior of the Moorish Palace.

[IBRAHIM *and* JUANINO *discovered;* IBRAHIM *seated Turkish fashion, and meditating.* JUANINO *stands near him.*]

JUANINO. Why, my Lord, are you always thus buried in grief?

IBRAHIM. You know well, Juanino, that for a long time the virtue of the Christians has made a deep impression on my heart. In secret, I have studied profoundly their sacred books; I have compared their dogmas with those of our Prophet; I have read, and I have doubted. (*Rises.*) I believe that our Mahomet was but a base impostor, whose only ambition was to tyrannize over his fellow-men,—an instrument of Heaven sent upon earth to punish the impiety of mortals! I believe that Christ is God; and that to Christians the sacred truths of Heaven have fallen as an inheritance.

JUANINO. Do not doubt it, my Lord; but my poor ignorance will only serve to compromise, in your eyes, the religion that I would defend. May I bring a holy priest to visit you? Disguised as an Arab, and an Infidel, he will gain admittance to your chamber. Question him. Make known to him your doubts; he will remove them, and illumine in you the light of true faith: he will crown my earthly desires in making you a Christian.

IBRAHIM. Know you not the laws that govern us?

JUANINO. I know, my Lord, that cruel tortures lie in store for me, if discovered.

IBRAHIM. But are there indeed priests among you?

JUANINO. They are ever to be found where there is good to be done.

IBRAHIM. And do they not fear the laws against them?

JUANINO. Life is nothing to them when a soul is at stake. Oh! if you had known them; if you had only seen them! Once before Toledo the army of Mahomet, under Tarik, took the Christians by surprise, and made us all prisoners.

We were thrown into a narrow dungeon, heaped one upon the other, deprived of all nourishment for whole days, or fed with garbage the swine would refuse. A devouring plague soon made its appearance in our midst. Our hearts were bowed down with grief; the sick expired writhing in the agonies of dark despair, cursing the life that God had given them, cursing Tarik who mocked them in their torments, and even cursing the Eternal Author of their being. With distorted features, eyes starting from their sockets, and bosoms palpitating with agony, devoured by an intolerable thirst that a few drops of stagnant water had only increased, we sat upon the corpses of our companions awaiting the dread moment when death should strike ourselves. Notwithstanding the horror of our miseries, everywhere vividly portrayed, our priests, hidden in the neighboring fields, knowing that in our midst were great sufferings to be alleviated, did not hesitate to seek an entrance into our dungeon. Why should they fear danger? Did not their Divine Master die for them? With gold they opened our prison doors; they consoled us in our grief; they calmed our sorrow, and reminded us that heaven would be the reward of our sufferings. Death's sting lost all its bitterness, slavery became sweet to us, and the pest quickly ceased its awful ravages. Strong, with God as our protector, and resigned to His laws, we bore with courage all the indignities that could be heaped upon us. But the vengeance of God was not yet satisfied, and Heaven chose another from us as its victim —one of our holy priests, worn out in his zeal for our eternal welfare. " My children," said he, a short time before his death, as he witnessed our grief, " why do you weep? why do you ask our Eternal Father to grant me, a miserable sinner, a longer life? Is it not sweet to give up life for a brother?" Thus do you find our priests: in the hour of danger they are never wanting.

IBRAHIM. Juanino, be my brother; I wish to become a Christian. From this moment, my only desire is to see the minister of the Most High. I wish to open my heart to him.

JUANINO. My Lord, persevere; your slave will go and find him.

IBRAHIM. Speak of slave, no longer, Juanino! You and I, henceforth, are brothers. Listen, now, to what I intend to do. You know my great influence in the palace; you know, too, the numerous friends I have outside its walls,

Well, then, these friends I wish to use to restore liberty to
the unfortunate Christians, whom yesterday the fortunes of
war placed in our hands. I know well to what evil influ-
ences they are exposed, and I wish to snatch them from the
dangers which menace them, and I myself will return with
them to their country. Go, prepare our arms. But, first,
tell me, Juanino, who is that cavalier who fought under our
flag and guided our soldiers against the Christians. His vizor
was lowered, and I could not see his features.

JUANINO. That man, whom Tarik has named Almanzor,
is the son of Gomez, one of the bravest cavaliers to whom
Spain has ever given birth. That is what I heard from one
of the slaves of the seraglio this morning.

IBRAHIM. What! this man a Christian, and fighting against
his brothers!

JUANINO. Alas, he is a Christian no longer, my Lord.
But, here comes Tarik; let us retire, my Lord, and devise
some means to rescue the Christians from the dangers that
threaten them. (*Exeunt*).

(*Enter* TARIK, ALONZO, *now called* ALMANZOR, *and*
LOPEZ).

TARIK. You have fought bravely, Almanzor! My eyes
did not leave you for an instant, and, without doubt, to you
belongs the honor of routing the infidels. May the blessing
of the Prophet be upon you! The success we have obtained
to-day must have but happy results. Pelagius, reduced to
his last resources, will soon be forced to submit; if he dares
to resist longer, we will pursue him into the midst of his
mountain fastnesses; we will track him like a wild beast into
the most inaccessible strongholds, and will efface proud,
haughty Spain from the number of Christian nations. Almanzor, your zeal merits a most worthy recompense. Your
noble birth entitled you to a throne which just now fell beneath your feet, and I, the lieutenant of the " Father of the
Faithful," wish to return to you what you have lost. The
kingdom of Murcia, conquered by our brave soldiers, awaits
a sovereign; go, Almanzor, place its crown upon your brow;
and, all honor to the King of Murcia!

ALONZO. My Lord, so much goodness——

TARIK. Should be repaid with a worthy devotedness.
To-morrow, Almanzor, you will go to take possession of

your crown; but, hark you! remember, the hand that conferred the crown can also take it again. Remember that, surrounded by the emissaries of Tarik, not one of your actions, nor a single thought, will be unknown to him. Reign justly, propagate the religion of Mahomet, and crush out Christianity. It is in the blood of Christian dogs you should blot out the cross imprinted by them on your forehead at your birth.

ALONZO. My Lord, the rank to which you deign to call me is sufficient, without doubt, to satisfy the most unbounded ambition; but, excuse my boldness, the open distrust which you show to me detracts much from the brilliance of the crown which you offer. And what! is not my honor pledged?

TARIK. Almanzor! Almanzor! he who denies his God has little honor! (ALONZO *starts*.) But throw aside these trivial griefs, which time will soften, and which emulous courtiers will soon cause you to forget. You know, Almanzor, the adversaries against whom you fought. Tell me the name of the warrior, in burnished armor, who wore a heavy helmet with jet-black plume, and who created such disorder in our ranks!

ALONZO. O God! I know too well!

TARIK. It was——

ALONZO. It was—my father!

TARIK. (*Smiling ironically*.) Your father! I congratulate you, Almanzor. He has fallen into our hands, and no doubt will find in you a powerful protector.

ALONZO. My Lord, it is now that I am entirely yours; it is now indeed that my treasures, my sword, my life belong to you. You will give my father his freedom, you will spare him all suffering?——

TARIK. You deceive yourself, Almanzor. You know the laws of the Prophet. I cannot infringe them: for the poor, slavery; for the noble, abjuration or death.

ALONZO. Death!

TARIK. But you, faithful believer, can easily prevail upon your father to cast aside your religion. You can employ about him all the means that filial affection may inspire. If the abjuration of the son merited a kingdom, judge what reward will be given to the father. I leave you, Almanzor, but will soon return to treat of the Murcian kingdom and our prisoners. (*Exit*).

ALONZO. A curse upon me! A curse upon the day that gave me birth! A curse upon all that surrounds me!—upon *you*, Lopez; upon you, who urged me on to the awful precipice, and plunged me headlong into the bottomless abyss of crime. Be thou too cursed, O fatal ambition! that has armed me against my father, against my country, and, oh, horror! against my God!

LOPEZ. (*Looking timidly about and speaking low.*) Speak low, my Lord; your loud voice may ruin us. Every passage of the palace is guarded by slaves who will hear us.

ALONZO. What care I for life, since all else, honor and name, are gone!

LOPEZ. In one instant we may lose the entire confidence of Tarik.

ALONZO. The confidence of Tarik! Did you not hear him say, Lopez, that he who denies his God has little honor? Do not these words strike you most forcibly? Do they not indicate at what a fearful price I have bought my kingdom? For it I have sacrificed religion, honor, country! I have given up my father to certain death. Oh! father, did you but know the warrior who led the infidel hosts was your only son, what agony would you not feel! He will not abjure his God; he will rather die; and 'tis I who have bowed his head beneath the scimitar! If he could not recognize me! Should he see me he would die of grief. (*Buries his face in his hands.*)

LOPEZ. Be calm, my Lord. I sympathize in your grief, but I understand how vain are your regrets. The curses with which you have loaded me do not astonish, nor do they terrify. Your blessings will take their place when you are at length securely seated on the throne of Murcia; and when surrounded by brave subjects, the master of untold treasures, you can defy with impunity the power of the caliphs, overturn their authority, and rise greater from their ruin.

ALONZO. Tarik was right; do you perceive it, Lopez? What cares he for an oath, who has no God? To him 'tis but an empty form of speech, that but a breath will scatter. You speak of Murcia, and your idea delights me, Lopez. Yes, let us be conspirators; let us overturn the power of those whose success lies solely in our hands. (*Noise of a whip.*) But what noise is that?

(*Enter* PEDRILLO, ABDALLAH, *and Spanish captives.*)

ABDALLAH. March on, dogs; march! (*Gives* PEDRILLO *a blow which makes him jump.*)

PEDRILLO. Ow! Take care, Mr. Mahometan; I've got a delicate skin, and your old whip hurts unmercifully; and, look here, if you don't quit I'll——

ABDALLAH. Silence, dog!

PEDRILLO. (*Aside.*) How ill-bred are these Mahometans! How strikingly good education is theirs!

ALONZO. (*Eagerly.*) Are these your only captives, Abdallah?

ABDALLAH. No, my Lord; these are but the rabble.

PEDRILLO. Well now, as I live, *this* is a farce! There's a Mahometan that looks for all the world like Don Alonzo, and the lantern-jawed creature with him must be Lopez.

ABDALLAH. (*To* PEDRILLO.) Is that your place, dog? (*Strikes him with whip.*)

PEDRILLO. (*Rubbing himself.*) Confound you, for a mule; to strike me who never touched you!

ABDALLAH. What do you say, dog?

PEDRILLO. I tell you again, I'm saying nothing. (*Aside.*) Big fool!

JUANINO. (*Enters.*) My Lord, the king of Murcia, and you, his trusted attendant, Tarik, the light of our eyes, the glory of the world, and the strength of the caliph, desires your presence. (*Exeunt* ALONZO, LOPEZ, *and* JUANINO.)

ABDALLAH. Dogs, stop here, and do not move a step till my return. I am going to receive the orders of my gracious master, Tarik. (*Exit*).

PEDRILLO. Yes, go and get your orders from the grand Tariff, but let them be to give us something to eat, for, zounds! I'm as hungry as a beggar, and haven't eaten anything since last night when I dined most humbly on a miserable roast sparrow. No wonder then I feel hungry—awfully hungry. (*To the other prisoners.*) Eh! And why do you stand there, with your thumbs in your mouths, and not a word nor a laugh out of you? I know, though, why you don't laugh; but then——

MARIETTO. Is slavery nothing to you, Pedrillo?

PEDRILLO. Well, it's not very amusing; but if one wears a most miserable countenance it will not change the affair. But, you see, if you were only men we could try to save ourselves; for myself, anyway, I'll start; there's no one near. Good-by!

JUANINO. (*Enters and stops* PEDRILLO.) You cannot pass!

PEDRILLO. And why not?

JUANINO. Because no one can pass, dog! (*Threatens* PEDRILLO *with sabre.*)

PEDRILLO. (*Frightened.*) O heavens! another of the cut-throats, who sport their big knives without regard to the fact that they might take a fellow's life! And that "Dog" again. It seems to me they know nothing but that. And it appears that when a person is taken a prisoner, he is free.

MARIETTO. Your idea is excellent, Pedrillo! Yes, we ought to endeavor to escape. What think you, comrades?

JUANINO. Silence, soldiers, a friend watches over you. If God favor our project we will soon rejoin Pelagius; but, if our days are numbered, rather die than live a tyrant's slaves!

MARIETTO. What say you, slave?

JUANINO. Sh-sh! Patience and courage! (*Exit.*)

MARIETTO. If Don Vasco was only with us, his courage and prudence——

PEDRILLO. Ah! that's true; he's a famous chap—this Don Vasco! Holy saint! when I saw him sweep down on those surly Mahometans and cleave their heads right through all the miserable wrappings twisted around them, I hid myself behind a bush to save my own.

MARIETTO. What! fled,—and you a Spaniard? Shame!

PEDRILLO. Yes, that's so. But, you see, when I'm alone I'm a regular lion for courage. Enemies! oh! if I had a dozen, a hundred of them now, I think I'd crush them; I'd pulverize them—grind them to atoms! But then when I get a look at them, I don't know why, yet, all at once, I feel as harmless as a poor old sheep. It's not funny, eh? But what——

MARIETTO. Some one is watching us; silence, babbler!

Comrades, let us appear resigned to our evil fortune! Mendoza, come, give us one of your stirring melodies.

MENDOZA. Yes, Marietto; gayety on our lips and burning rage within our hearts.

Oh! what to us is Dame Fortune's deceit;
    Gay soldiers like us can laugh at her wiles;
And our jokes can our laughter repeat,
    And mock at her tears and her smiles.

II.

But when Vengeance' dread day doth appear,
    Like men made of steel we'll arise,
Our lances with gore we'll besmear
    And the rage of proud tyrants despise.

III.

But yester'n Spain's soldier was I;
    A slave of the Sultan to-day;
In slavery no change I descry—
    What matters it whom I obey!

IV.

For honors and wealth let men sigh,
    It may pain them to see them all vanish;
But we, with our hearts beating high,
    Far away every care we shall banish.
      Fra-la-la-la; la-la-la; la-la-la;
      Fra-la-la-la; la-la-la; la-la-la!

PEDRILLO. By my faith it is truly nice, this song (*shouts*): La-la-la-la. (*Enter* ABDALLAH, ALONZO, *and* LOPEZ.)

ABDALLAH. Silence, dogs! (*To* ALONZO.) I go, my Lord, to bring hither the prisoner I hold confined. *Exit*.)

ALONZO. And this is Tarik's desire! Seduce my father! Oh! if I could disguise myself beneath these garments; if I could keep from him my name,—hide my birth! Vain delusions! Disguise myself from my father! Oh, awful moment! Can I dare to look upon him! Yet I must; for 'tis I alone can save him!—save him! Abjuration or death! Oh, God! I hear his footsteps; whither can I fly! (*Enter* ABDALLAH *and* DON VASCO.)

ABDALLAH. This way, prisoner; Lord Almanzor waits to speak with you.

DON VASCO. Let him speak.

ALONZO. (*With averted head.*) Fortune, my Lord, has proved very unfavorable to you.

DON VASCO. Great God! that voice!—those features!——

ALONZO. Are the features of your son.

DON VASCO. (*Surprised.*) No; my eyes deceive me! A deceitful phantasm imposes upon me! You cannot be the son of Gomez! He never wore the turban of the Arabs! He never clothed himself with the *insignia* of Mahometanism! Begone, impostor! and, if to tempt me you have brought the features of my son to your aid, you will not succeed.

ALONZO. My Lord, hear me. Think of your own life and mine.

DON VASCO. Spaniards, approach! Behold this man! He is at liberty, and I am in chains! he is a Mahometan, and I am a Christian, and he calls himself my son! Do you believe him?

ALONZO. Father!

DON VASCO. Impostor, profane not that name! I *your* father! Great God! were it so, I would say " miserable wretch! are you my son, and dare you present yourself before me covered with the livery of infamy!" But you do not know that I would call upon you the wrath of God! No, you are not my son! Your features, your voice, are those of Alonzo, and your carriage is his. But your name is Almanzor. Your faith is not mine. My sovereign is Pelagius; yours, the leader of the cursed tribe of Mahomet,—and you call yourself my son! Speak, Almanzor; your prisoner listens.

ALONZO. My Lord, why do you maintain this apparent ignorance? Why do you seem to doubt that I am your son?

DON VASCO. You wish it, Almanzor; therefore I consent. Be then my son. But thus the *rôles* are changed, and you will listen while I speak. Son of Gomez, listen then, and answer the inquiries of your judge.

ALONZO. Slaves, withdraw.

DON VASCO. No, their place is here! They are all Spaniards, and are not slaves.

ALONZO. But, my Lord, will you humiliate me before them?

Don Vasco. If you are not my son, what signifies their presence? But, if you are, then should you be proud to stand in their midst! Never, in the history of our fathers, has a Gomez been known to be afraid to speak with perfect freedom, and never has he blushed before his own. Again, I say, if you are my son, answer me, then, your father. Let not the presence of these noble Spaniards bind your tongue; before them you must justify yourself. What do you do, how came you here, and why linger in this den of iniquity? Whence comes all your power? Tell me, O son of Gomez, tell me, where is your grand old faith? and why, deserting the banner of Pelagius, are you found commanding the legions of infidel Tarik?

Alonzo. This, my Lord, is not the moment for a reply. An imminent danger threatens you; your lot is cast between abjuration and death.

Don Vasco (*calmly*). Think you my choice is doubtful?

Alonzo. My Lord, for the sake of your son, you must abjure your God.

Don Vasco (*coolly*). I must abjure! Indeed! And what, then, would be the reward of my criminal compliance?

Alonzo. (*Aside.*) He is won! (*Aloud.*) Power, honor and, perhaps, a crown.

Don Vasco. And you, who call yourself my son, what have you received?

Alonzo. I am king of Murcia.

Don Vasco. Behold, then, the mystery. (*Rises ironically.*) Hail, king of Murcia! Hail, son of Gomez! (*Indignantly.*) O Heaven! what am I saying? Wretch, you bear my name, and can behold without a blush the shame of your aged father! Soldiers, take me away! there is not the shadow of a tie between this man and me; take me away, I say!

Alonzo. My Lord!

Don Vasco. Take me away!

Alonzo. (*Falling at his feet.*) My Lord, at your feet behold your unhappy son.

Don Vasco. Cease, wretch, to call yourself thus. Do you wish to be my son? Break, then, your tinsel crown; trample beneath your feet that hateful turban; cry out aloud: "I am a

Christian; I abhor Mahomet; I curse his birth!" But you do not speak; you cringe at my feet, and lick their dust.

ALONZO. Too late! my Lord; it is now too late!

DON VASCO. Too late, infamous wretch! Begone, serpent! that I have nourished but to destroy me. Take from me my feeble remnant of life that I may never more behold your hated countenance. Traitor to your God, be you cursed by him as by your heart-broken father. (*Exit.* ALONZO *falls on his face.*)

ALL. Great God! (*Enter* LOPEZ.)

LOPEZ. (*Raising* ALONZO.) My Lord, arise; away from this rabble! We will again endeavor to calm his wrath.

ALONZO. (*Looks about bewildered.*) Ah! 'tis you, my dear Lopez. My father has cursed me, and his anathema has penetrated the marrow of my bones. Where is my father? He has not yet been put to death? What do you wish, Tarik? I was the son of Gomez, but thou call'st me Amanzor. I am king of Murcia! Let the people offer me homage. Prostrate at my feet, I wish to behold them from the summit of my throne. What have I said, Lopez? Ha, ha, ha! (*Laughs wildly.*) Have you seen Pelagius? I will bathe myself in his vile blood; I will plunge my hand into the depths of his entrails; I will crush his hoary head. How beautiful are the heavens; Mahomet alone is great! Why, then, Abdallah, did you not efface these crosses from the walls? I was also a Christian! Why does this awful cross arise before my eyes? I see—I see the Immaculate Virgin trampling the crescent beneath her feet—and now! oh, hence! awful vision; hence! Ah! Lopez, do you see the hand that threatens me? You, also, does it menace. Come! away! Let us flee?—O God! upon the air, upon the walls, upon my heart is written : "Cursed! cursed! cursed!" (*Exeunt* ALONZO *and* LOPEZ.)

PEDRILLO. Ha, ha! there's not much fun there. But what did he want to make so many faces for? and then cry out that he saw something most horrible? I don't see anything written on the walls. I think he's either crazy or drunk.

ABDALLAH. That's very well, but it's none of your business. (*To the prisoners.*) Come here, dogs!

PEDRILLO. (*Aside.*) Well, he is an unmannerly rascal. Oh! you ugly thief, if ever I get you in a pinch, and nobody but the two of us there—God help you!

ABDALLAH. My sovereign lord, the pearl of the East, the conqueror Tarik, is on his way hither. You have your choice: Be Mahometans, or work in the mines. Come, come! decide quickly!

ALL. We choose the mines.

ABDALLAH. Hey! You do not think of what you do!

ALL. We are all Christians.

ABDALLAH. Five hundred lashes for the first who dares again to pronounce that name.

PEDRILLO. (*Aside.*) They don't know how to count unless by five hundred! But perhaps there is a means of making it good.

ABDALLAH. You have considered?

ALL. Yes, yes!

PEDRILLO. That is——

ABDALLAH. What?

PEDRILLO. That is, my Lord Abradra,——that is,—— that——

ABDALLAH. Do you know that my patience is sorely tried, and I wouldn't hesitate to lop off your head for the pleasure of sharpening my cimitar.

PEDRILLO. Gently, gently, Lord Abraca. (*Aside.*) The old fool speaks only of cutting and chopping as if he took poor suffering humanity for an old pumpkin.

ABDALLAH. Will you be quick?

PEDRILLO. Yes, yes, my Lord; don't get angry. I wished to say if it was convenient to arrange our affair nicely and friendly between us two, as they say, that——that——

ABDALLAH. Well!

PEDRILLO. Well, yes; that if, instead of sending me to the mines—for, you see, that wouldn't suit me at all, because they say there is no light there, and, in fact, the light and I have always been accustomed to live together; that one without the other—that is, that one after the other—that one for the other—yes, just so, you understand——

ABDALLAH. Yes, I understand that my patience is all gone. Do you wish to become a Mahometan or remain a Christian. Come, speak!

PEDRILLO. Well, you know, if there were any means of

being a Mahometan and remaining a Christian at the same
time, that would suit me pretty well; something just in the
middle of the two; eh!——

ABDALLAH. Back, dog! Behold the great Tarik approaching.

(*Enter* TARIK *with* LOPEZ, *now called* SOLIMAN.)

TARIK. What say you, Soliman? I cannot believe it:
Almanzor insane!

LOPEZ. He is, my Lord. His father, driven on by anger,
poured upon him a most crushing anathema. Thunder-
stricken by the words of malediction, we saw him fall to the
earth. After raising him, he at first seemed to find himself
surrounded by crosses, and then the exclamation " Cursed! "
became ever present to his disordered sight. But, my Lord,
the throne of Murcia is again vacant, Almanzor can no
longer think or act; and, if you would deign to confer it upon
me——

TARIK. *I* give you a kingdom, Lopez! Are you mad!

LOPEZ. Great devotedness,—a zeal beyond every proof,
—a strict observance of the laws of Mahomet,—a——

TARIK. A strict observance of the laws of Mahomet!
You astonish me, Lopez. You, a good Mahometan! No;
I do not believe it.

LOPEZ. Is it necessary, my Lord, to prove my devotedness?

TARIK. I believe you capable of trampling on the Cross,
of desecrating the churches, and of burning the sacred shrines
of the Christians. You were always, I know, a very bad
Christian, but a good Mahometan! I doubt it very much.
Think you, you can deceive me? Believe you that I have
grown old in observing, without knowing the nature of men?
Your god is ambition; your faith, nothing,—and you ask a
throne! Foolish man! A traitor to your God, a traitor to
your king,—are you then worthy to wear a crown? Listen,
Lopez, and know that a traitor is a villain who parts with his
faith at the first favorable opportunity; whom one caresses
while he suits his purpose, but throws aside, when useless, as
a bruised and broken reed.

LOPEZ. Nevertheless, Alonzo, too, was a traitor.

TARIK. Think you I respect him?

LOPEZ. He had a kingdom.

TARIK. But he sprang from a family of kings, and could longer serve our interests. Do you know that, Lopez, or rather Soliman? And, now, do you wish me to read your thoughts? You long to betray us.

LOPEZ. Who told you that, my lord?

TARIK. Who told me! My good judgment,—your face, —your embarrassment,—your interest,—your past conduct! But you are constantly watched.

LOPEZ. Tarik, beware!

TARIK. Cease your mean insolence; I will spit upon your vile carcass. Soldiers, watch him carefully.

LOPEZ. Behold my reward. (*A slave enters.* TARIK *motions to* LOPEZ *to withdraw.*)

SLAVE. (*To* TARIK, *in a low voice.*) Light of our eyes, a plot is formed to deliver the infidels whom you have taken prisoners. Guard yourself, my lord. God alone is great and Mahomet is His prophet!

TARIK. A plot! Ah, well! I'll foil their project.

ALONZO. (*Enters.*) I have been looking for you, Tarik. Do you know he has cursed me?——You know my father? He will not abjure his God; he will die for his faith. If you wish, Tarik, take back your kingdom. I will not be a king any longer. I am Pelagius. Come, let us all adore the Cross. Look, father, I have returned to the faith; I am a Christian. Father, clasp me once again to your paternal heart!——

TARIK. Back, fool!

ALONZO. 'Tis true, I'm cursed, cursed!

TARIK. (*Reflecting.*) I must overthrow their plot. If I could only win this obstinate old man to our cause! I must question him; if he resist, let him die! What! But what is the blood of an infidel to me! Abdallah, let Don Vasco appear! (TARIK *seats himself. Enter* DON VASCO. *Guards surround him.*)

DON VASCO. You seek in vain to terrify me.

TARIK. Silence! You will speak when I question you.

DON VASCO. I am ready.

TARIK. Why, abusing your power over your vassals, have you engaged them to fight against the soldiers of the true God?

DON VASCO. The true God is not He of whom Mahomet has spoken.

TARIK. Why have you yourself borne aloft a proscribed banner, and stricken the only true believers?

DON VASCO. Those whom I have stricken are miscreants; they are the enemies of my country and my faith.

TARIK. Who are you who speak to me thus?

DON VASCO. I am Don Vasco de Gomez, a Spaniard and a Christian.

TARIK. Know you my power? Know you who I am?

DON VASCO. You may kill me; your name is Tarik; you have covered my unhappy country with ruins; you are drenched with the purest blood of Spain; your soldiers are cruel brigands, and you,—you are their chief.

TARIK. Wretched slave, do you dare to insult me?

DON VASCO. There is no slavery for a Christian.

TARIK. I will tear out your tongue, and destroy your eyes!

DON VASCO. What care I for my body, if I but save my soul?

TARIK. Senseless man! Vasco, reflect a moment. Listen: —join our ranks and save your life.

DON VASCO. Life is nothing to me.

TARIK. You will live surrounded by a world of wealth and honors.

DON VASCO. Will earthly honors follow me to heaven?

TARIK. You will gain a crown.

DON VASCO. Is it as brilliant as that which my God reserves for His elect?

TARIK. Your faith is folly.

DON VASCO. That folly has saved the world.

TARIK. You think, perhaps, obstinate old man as you are, that a speedy death will give you, without pain, that crown that your fanatic zeal promises you. But you are mistaken. I will crush your proud spirit with the greatest tortures; I will place you on a funeral pyre, and, having caused you to suffer a thousand torments, I will burn your body to a cinder upon the slowest of fires.

DON VASCO. I am a Christian!

TARIK. Yield, miserable man! Continue obstinate, and I will throw the whole troop of these thy companions to the fury of the bloody executioner.

DON VASCO. Spaniards, what is your counsel?

ALL. We are Christians.

TARIK. Dogs! you shall all die! Guards, away with them! (*To* DON VASCO.) You also shall die! Upon your torn and bleeding heart I will vent my rage. Cry aloud " Cursed be Christ," or die!

DON VASCO. Must I again repeat, Tarik, " I am a Christian!"

TARIK. Away to the torture with him!

ALONZO. (*Throwing himself towards* DON VASCO.) My father! Oh! where do you drag him?

TARIK. To death!

DON VASCO. (*Repelling* ALONZO.) To eternal glory!

(ABDALLAH *and* SOLDIERS *surround* DON VASCO, *who walks slowly, but with firm step, and head erect.*)

TABLEAU.

ACT THIRD.

Village of Asturia.

SCENE I.

(FABRICIO, PEDRO *and* PEASANTS.)

PEDRO. Rejoice, my good friends. Pelagius has defeated the Mahometans again. The soldiers of Tarik, continually opposed and pursued, abandon their conquests. God is for us, my good friends, and protects our beloved Spain. Fabricio, go draw a bottle of our finest wine, that we may drink to the success of our arms and the return of my poor Pedrillo, for whose safety I begin to fear.

FABRICO. Yes, that's so. To the return of my brother Pedrillo I'll go and open a bottle of wine, but of the best kind I know.

PEDRO. Well, hurry up, you lazy rascal.

FABRICIO. Hurry up! faster; don't you see I'm running. (*Exit very slowly.*)

(*Enter* ALONZO *at the back of the stage, clothed grotesquely, ragged, with pale face and haggard eyes.*)

PEDRO. (*Addressing* ALONZO.) Come, my poor fellow; come you too and be merry, if it be possible for you. Well, one must indeed be very unhappy when he has so far lost his reason as not to know that he is spoken to. (ALONZO *approaches without speaking.*)

FABRICIO. (*Returning.*) Here it is; and famous wine, too. (*To the* PEASANTS.) Come on, friends. Oh! here he is again—that fellow, with his awful eyes! He frightens me whenever I look at him.

ALONZO. (*To* PEDRO.) Good day, father. I am very hungry.

PEDRO. You will have something to eat, then, my poor boy.

FABRICIO. Yes, yes, just like you, father; not a poor old beggar comes along but must eat our bread.

ALONZO. (*To* FABRICIO.) You never knew hunger, young man! You were never weary and faint, dying for a morsel of bread. You are light-hearted and happy.

FABRICIO. I'm never hungry! Certainly; I'm always, when I'm a good while without anything to eat. But that is not a reason that——

ALONZO. That I am hungry; is it not?

FABRICIO. Certainly; any one——

PEDRO. Silence, Fabricio; respect the misery of this poor man! Come, Fernando; come, my boy, stop with me. I'm not rich, but while our good Lord and the Mahometans leave me a crust of bread, you will share it with me.

FABRICIO. Yes, just so! And what will you do with your own children?

PEDRO. Be quiet, I tell you!

FABRICIO. But——

PEDRO. Silence! or I'll pull your ears.

FABRICIO. (*To* ALONZO.) Oh! you'll pay for this, you crazy fool! Why didn't you stay at home in your kingdom, you ugly beggar? (PEDRO *steps toward him, and* FABRICIO *runs away.*)

ALONZO. True, why did I leave my kingdom! (*To* PEDRO.) What! Lopez, you near me! Where are my courtiers? Let pleasure reign throughout the palace! Call my slaves! Away; prepare a gorgeous banquet, and let the merry laugh resound throughout our halls! For you know, Lopez, my heart is broken and I am forever miserable! Why are these walls draped with black? Bah! Begone, Lopez! I am going back to my father! Hark! hear his footsteps echoing through that vaulted passage-way! There, there, I see his shining armor! He approaches,—he commands me to stand. I will obey! Father, I stand,—but approach, approach. Father, come and bless thy son. O God! I see but a horrible spectre, that trembles with rage, that shakes its galling chains and menaces me with its fleshless finger (*falls on his knees*). Father! oh, father, do not leave me! do not abandon me! (*Screams.*) Oh! no, no! do not curse me! (*Falls on the ground.*)

PEDRO. Fabricio! Fabricio!

FABRICIO. (*Stretching in his head from the side.*) What is it, father?

PEDRO. Some water, quick!

FABRICIO. (*Advancing.*) Is he dead? I'm glad of it!

PEDRO. Rascal! (ALONZO *rises and presses his forehead.*)

FABRICIO. It's not so bad. Look, father, he is getting up; such men don't die in a hurry.

ALONZO. (*To* FABRICIO.) Infamous Tarik! at last I have found you! It was your seductions that plunged me into the abyss. 'Twas you who caused me to renounce my God, and He has punished me,—for I am mad! mad! But you shall die. I will bury my sharpened poniard in your bosom; I will pierce your heart, and I will tear your body with my teeth. Ah, ha! you tremble,—you flee! Oh, you will not escape me! (*While he speaks,* FABRICIO *runs about the stage, and* ALONZO *follows him.* FABRICIO *falls on his knees.*)

FABRICIO.   Oh! pardon, Mr. Fernando, but I'm not called Carrott.   I only know that he is———

ALONZO.   True, you are too wicked to permit of my stain-ing my sword with your blood.

FABRICIO.   Oh, yes! do not soil your sword, I beseech you.

PEDRO.   My dear Fernando,—poor child!—come to your repose again.   See how beautiful all nature is; how green the trees and how bright and sparkling the waters.

ALONZO.   'Tis your voice, father!   Oh, how warm I am! Why am I dressed so!   Fabricio, why are you terrified?

FABRICIO.   No wonder I'd be afraid, when you, with your antics, have chilled every drop of blood in me; so that———

ALONZO.   My God! my God! did I fall again into a fit of madness.   Pardon me, Fabricio.

FABRICIO.   Oh! it's easy enough to say pardon, pardon! But when you had killed me; when you had eaten my heart with a little salt, would I pardon you then?   Perhaps!

ALONZO.   (*To* PEDRO.)   Father—for you merit that name —you, alone, have pity on me; when all abandoned me, you stretched forth your hand to my assistance; when all repulsed me, you received me and appeased my hunger.

FABRICIO.   And without reproaching you for being aw-fully hungry.

ALONZO.   I ask yet another morsel of bread for to-day, as I am very hungry.   But, then, I will leave you; I will bury myself in the caverns of yonder mountains, where I may be able to end the miseries of this wretched life.   Here, perhaps, I might be forced to repay your unbounded generosity with crime.

FABRICIO.   Yes, indeed, this is good reasoning, I say.

PEDRO.   I am going to give you bread, my child, not only to-day, but to-morrow, and always.   Fabricio, quick! some bread and wine.

FABRICIO.   But, father——

PEDRO.   Go, I say!   (*To* ALONZO.)   Fernando, but one thing troubles me,—you will not tell me your name.

ALONZO. Impossible!

PEDRO. Why impossible, my boy? At present, while your mind is calm, you can make known to me your sorrows and sufferings. I am but a poor peasant; but what of that! I may perhaps be able to give you some consolation in your affliction. Come, my boy, tell me your name.

ALNOZO. I cannot; if I tell you my name, I shall lose your esteem. I do not wish to appear to you otherwise than a poor unfortunate, and I fear to show myself a criminal.

PEDRO. But you belong to a more elevated rank than mine; your language, your manners, are not those of the common people; you must belong to some noble family.

ALONZO. I have none; I have renounced it.

PEDRO. And your father?

ALONZO. My father! I have one no longer. But, oh! cease these questions. I feel——my head——is becoming troubled again. Pedro, my benefactor, my ideas are confused; my heart is broken. Oh, unfortunate creature that I am!

PEDRO. My child, my child, I respect your secret; I will no longer seek to know it. But why does Fabricio not come? Come, come, Fernando; come, quench your thirst and appease your hunger; a short repose will calm your agitated mind; come. (*Exeunt. Enter* FABRICIO *with a basket on his arm.*)

FABRICIO. Well, well! Where can they have gone now? Father! Fernando! no one answers! Father! Father! Not a word. Who knows but Fernando, with his old kingdom, has carried my father off with him! I don't know; but I always had the idea that this man, with his Carik and Lopez, might be either a sorcerer or the devil changed into a Christian to cut up some of his capers. I——I——I——don't know why, but I shiver like a leaf, and big drops of sweat are oozing out of my forehead; just look at them. I'm afraid to go back alone. Oh, oh, oh! (*Enter* PEDRILLO *running.*)

PEDRILLO. Here I am at last!

FABRICIO. (*Frightened.*) Father, father! help! the devil!

PEDRILLO. What! are you a fool? Keep quiet. (*Approaches.*)

FABRICIO. (*Recoiling.*) Not so near, Mr. Sa—Sa—Satan, ——Mr. Bee—Beel—Beelzebub, I beg of you.

PEDRILLO. Well, this is pleasant! Can I have grown like the devil without knowing it? What! Fabricio, don't you know me?

FABRICIO. Do I know you?—don't come near me. O Lord! what claws he has!

PEDRILLO. (*Frightened.*) Am I really like the devil, Fabricio? Am I truly the devil?

FABRICIO. Is it true? and you with your big horns and awful eyes!

PEDRILLO. Horns! eyes! claws! that's funny. I don't see them. But, Fabricio,——

FABRICIO. Shut up! " Get thee behind me, Satan."

PEDRILLO. Again you tell me I've become the devil! Well, I won't doubt it; but I know I haven't got claws. My nails are a little too long—that's all. But, Fabricio. (*Approaches.*)———

FABRICIO. Father! Father! Help! help!

PEDRO. (*Entering.*) What!—What is it?—Where are they? Where? What! Good Lord! is it you, my poor Pedrillo?

PEDRILLO. Don't come near me, father! they say I'm the devil!

PEDRO. Are you crazy too?

PEDRILLO. There's one of us crazy, but I don't know which.

FABRICIO. Father, is this my brother Pedrillo?

PEDRO. Who else could it be?

FABRICIO. (*Embracing.*) Oh, my poor brother! and I took you for the devil!

PEDRILLO. I'm not his infernal majesty any longer, then? Well, so much the better, for I have but little regard for him.

PEDRO. But I can't understand what—

FABRICIO. Look here, father; I was thinking entirely of this fool Fernando, and I took it into my head that he was the devil; then Pedrillo appeared, and I thought surely *he* was Satan himself.

PEDRO. You are both crazy.

PEDRILLO. All right, father; I'm used to it now, and this is nothing new to me.

PEDRO. What will you have me say, then; am I not right? But, come, my boy, let me embrace you once more—you whom I thought long since dead.

PEDRILLO. Well, if I am not dead, certainly I came more than once near dying. But, say father, my throat is as dry as an oven, and I'd like to have a little something just to give me breath.

FABRICIO. (*Showing basket.*) I've got something here, Pedrillo; a bottle of famous wine——Hold on!——there, take a good drink of it.

PEDRILLO. (*Drinking*). Ah! um! good! Better than all the compliments of the Mahometans, who, I assure you, are most miserably brought up. But now, let us sit down here and keep silence.

FABRICIO. Keep silence, when I'm forever silent; when I have truly lost my tongue and speech. So that——

PEDRILLO. There, there, there! You see, though, you're always talking, and if you keep on I can't speak myself.

FABRICIO. All right, Pedrillo; all right. Go on!

PEDRILLO. I am on the point—just a little drop (*drinks*). So that—you remember—it was the day the Mahometans invaded our little village. You, father, were with our good peasants, and fought bravely. I don't like to praise myself, but there are only brave soldiers in the family; yes, I know that.

PEDRO. Go on, Pedrillo.

PEDRILLO. All right. Fabricio hid himself under a stack of hay, to keep out of danger. By chance I was left alone in the house, when, all of a sudden, the door burst open with a crash. I didn't lose a second but jumped immediately to the foot of the stairs, and, grabbing by the legs the first Mahometan I met, I threw him over my head, and, slap-bang! used him right and left like a good stout club, and terrified all that saw me. After I killed about two hundred and seventy-seven, I set the fellow on his legs again, and let him go; of course, he didn't ask for anything better, but ran for his life. Worn out with fatigue, I wiped the sweat from my forehead, when a troop of horsemen—about ten thousand—surrounded me, and I was obliged to surrender. As everybody knows, there is no use resisting force. They took me before the Mahometan general, and he at first view, said to me, " Dog!" For you see, father, when they want to pay any one a compliment they always say that " dog!"

PEDRO. Well, go on, Pedrillo. What next? We know how you were made prisoner of Tarik. Now we want to know your adventures after that.

PEDRILLO. All right, father; all right! but you'll spoil it all if you be in such a hurry. I was afterwards taken to prison, and from there brought before the great Tarik; and then, another great adventure! Whom should I meet but Lord Alonzo, who had become a Mahometan, and obtained a kingdom; and had, of course, I suppose, become a king! Then his father Don Vasco recognized him, and after a long dispute, said to him: "You are not my son!" Then the son answered, " It is not true, I am your son and you are my father!" Then the father became very angry, and the son threw himself at his feet. But the father cried—" You are an apostate; I curse you!" and then the son fell on his face and turned insane.

PEDRO and FABRICIO. Turned insane!

PEDRILLO. Yes, went crazy! So much so, that when he got up, he didn't know what he said, and spoke only of his kingdom.

FABRICIO. Eh? Spoke only of his kingdom?

PEDRILLO. He took everybody for different persons, always saw crosses, and——

PEDRO and FABRICIO. It's he!

PEDRILLO. Who's he?

PEDRO. Go on. Go on with your story.

PEDRILLO. A little while after, they tried to make us all Mahometans. But there's where I was solid, though. Renounce my God! What did they take me for! When they said to me, " Dog, curse your Christ!" I replied: "I am a Christian." Did they recommence the same song, I again would give them the air. Don Vasco, who was there, encouraged by *my* firmness, boldly replied to the same questions; one and all did the same, and we were all condemned to death.

PEDRO. My poor Pedrillo!

PEDRILLO. Behold us, then, dead!

FABRICIO. Hey?

PEDRILLO. When I say dead, I don't exactly mean that, though we were not quite alive. Hear now how we succeeded escaping from death. We had been brought outside of the city, in the first place, to be beheaded. On each side of us were bodies of Mahometans, as a guard of honor. They were boasting of how they would rejoice and laugh to see us walking without needing a cap, when—listen, now—when, whoop! down went a Mahometan head first to the ground. Marietto, a prisoner, had freed him from the troubles of life by plunging into his throat a stilletto. that he had carried concealed. He then grasped the arms of the dead man; all the prisoners threw themselves on the Mahometans; the Mahometans on the prisoners,—and, oh! what a bedlam! such confusion! Here, noses and eyes were flying around; there, heads that preferred to stay on their owners' shoulders; others rolling in the dust,—and, of the latter, I made a great number myself. Grasping a lance, I pierced about six of the most valiant of the enemy. A body of masked horsemen approached quickly, on hearing the noise of the conflict, and fell upon the Arabs who ran for dear life,—one, without an arm; another, a leg; and others lamenting their heads, that they had left on the field of battle. Oh, I never saw such a horrible sight! And if you could have only got a bird's-eye view of me, father, just to see how I fought them, and how they ran like a flock of frightened sheep. Oh, the villains! the cowards! If I only had twenty-five of them here now,—no: fifty, or a hundred. Oh! how nervous I get when I think that if——
(*Enter* GENSARO *running.*)

GENSARO. Pedro, quick! To arms! The Mahometans! (*Signs of fear on the faces of* PEDRILLO *and* FABRICIO.)

PEDRO. Run, children, run! To arms! Come, let us die, if necessary, for Pelagius and God. What? You will not follow! One would say you are both afraid.

PEDRILLO. I afraid! No, indeed; I'm not afraid! If I have any fear at all it is only through motives of humanity, lest the enemy would turn into figures of stone on beholding me. I wish I could find a little corner to hide in, but only through a motive of humanity.

PEDRO. Pedrillo, you're a coward! (*Exeunt* PEDRO and FABRICIO.)

PEDRILLO. I didn't say I wasn't, father. But—I hear some one coming—oh! where will I hide? Oh, heavens! and I have only just escaped from those awful Mahometans. May God protect me! Ah, here under this bench! (*Hides under the bench.*)

(*Enter* DON VASCO, MARIETTO, *and* SOLDIERS.)

DON VASCO. Rest for a while, my brave fellows! we are at last in a country of friends. May God be praised! We were not worthy of the noble crown of martyrdom. He wishes to try us a few years longer in this miserable world. May His holy will be done!

PEDRILLO. (*Under the bench.*) That's funny! who ever heard before Mahometans talking like Christians! If I only dared to look at them!

DON VASCO. No one appears. We must know where Pelagius is stationed. Marietto, seek some of the inhabitants and bring them with you; I will await your return. (*Seats himself on the bench. The* SOLDIERS *lie down.*) Sleep weighs down my eyelids; ten nights, passed without repose, have weakened my strength. I am nearly exhausted. O God, watch over me! Guard my son! protect my son, whom I have cursed! (*Rises agitated.*) Yes, and whom I will curse forever, if he remains an apostate. (*Sits again.*) My son, that I loved so much— that I love yet, even while cursing him in his evil course! (*Falls asleep.*)

PEDRILLO. I don't hear any noise (*stretches out his head*). They are all asleep. Just wait a while then, my friends, and I'll profit by it. (*Comes out from beneath the bench; walks towards the side on his tip-toes, and is about to go off the stage when* MARIETTO *appears and seizes him by the collar.*)

MARIETTO. Stand, traitor!

PEDRILLO. (*Frightened.*) It isn't me, I tell you; it isn't me! (*All the* SOLDIERS *arise.*)

MARIETTO. What! is it you, you fool?

PEDRILLO. Surely every one in Spain will have me by that name soon.

DON VASCO. Ha, a spy! Who is this man?

MARIETTO. He is but a miserable coward, my Lord.

PEDRILLO. A coward! ha, ha! that's something new.

Just as if a fellow is a coward because he gets scared once in a while.

DON VASCO. What news, Marietto?

MARIETTO. My lord, all the peasants are in arms; they are stationed on the neighboring mountain, and will not let me approach.

PEDRILLO. They will let me approach, a proof that I'm not a coward. If you will let me go, Lord Vasco, I will bring you the news. Oh, I'm a coward! Look out, there! Let me pass. (*Exit.*)

(*Enter* ALONZO *running across the stage.*)

DON VASCO. O Heavens! my son! Soldiers, bring him to me!

ALONZO. Hold, rash men! have you forgotten who I am? who you are? Could Tarik forget his promises? has he forgotten what I did for him! (*To* DON VASCO.) You, who seem to command these men, tell me who I am.

DON VASCO. What! Alonzo——

ALONZO. You call me Alonzo, who told you my name? My father used to call me that. I was a Christian then; but, times are changed. My name is Almanzor; I am king of Murcia; Mahomet is the prophet of God. You do not speak, friend?

DON VASCO. O God! I have lost my son, my only son!

ALONZO. Old man, you weep! And I weep also. You weep for your son, and I for my father. Was your boy also called Alonzo? It is the name of an outcast,—of a being poor and cursed!

DON VASCO. Alonzo, my boy, 'tis I, your father.

ALONZO. You jest, old man! I killed my father! He died for his God; but I renounced my own father. Long, long ago, with him, an humble child of Mary, I adored the God of Hosts. I was happy then, but I wished to be a king. I envied Pelagius; I sold all to become avenged,—I sold my honor, and I sold my country. I sacrificed all--all to the demon of pride: my God, my king, my father, and a happy eternity!—eternity! Let me reflect, old man,—what has so great a sacrifice gained for me! (*He seems buried in profound reflection.*)

DON VASCO. Unhappy Alonzo! Is there no more time for you to repent? God has taken away the reason that ought to guide you, which alone you ought to cherish, which caused your pride. Oh, unhappy child!

ALONZO. Speak, speak, old man! I know not why your voice is sweet. Oh! I enjoy such happiness in hearing it! Call me Alonzo; say to me, "I am your father!"

DON VASCO. My son, you break my heart! Return to me; return to reason,—your father begs you! O God, if forty years passed in Thy service have deserved any reward; if my blood poured out in defence of Thy Name; if I have long borne chains and braved the scaffold, oh! return my boy to life; restore to him that light which each one bears within himself, which guides our actions, which causes us to merit Thy boundless love or hate; give him back the reason which Thou hast snatched from him, by which he may again be led to repentance, and repair with his blood—repair with his life, the crime he has committed in renouncing his faith.

ALONZO. You pray for me, old man, and you call yourself my father! But *he* cursed me! I am worthy of his hate.

DON VAS. Return to me, my son, and I will bless you! Abjure your errors, curse the impious sect, which, for a moment, bound you in its ties. Repeat, " Glory to Christ! all honor to His holy law!" and your pardon, my son, will descend from the throne of the Almighty. Open your eyes to the true light, and your heart to repentance.

ALONZO. Stop a moment! My head is bursting. What! all is changed! Do I dream? Are these all Spanish soldiers? O heavens! my father! Father! Father! oh, do not curse me! I will die at your feet (*falls before* DON VASCO).

DON VASCO. Rise, son of Gomez, and say: "I am a Christian."

ALONZO. Yes, father, I am a Christian; cursed be Mahomet! May the thunders of God's vengeance annihilate his followers. May——

DON VASCO. My son, to God alone leave the care of vengeance; He, alone, is all-powerful.

(*Cries of " To the rescue! to the rescue!" " The Mahometans!" are heard outside.*) *Enter* PEDRILLO, *running.*

PEDRILLO. There, there! in the valley! Chase them, Lord Vasco! chase them!

DON VASCO. Comrades, to arms! Let us fight the infidels!

ALONZO. No, father, stay you here: I wish to lead them. Spaniards, follow me; in your van I will either check the enemy or die for my God. *Exeunt.*)

DON VASCO. Yes: go, my son; repair your fault; defend your country, and spare not your blood in its defence. I feel I am growing old and feeble; I could not follow you. Let us rest here; my head is confused. Peasant, look up yonder; do you see the battle?

PEDRILLO. Yes, yes, I see them! O God! how they fight!—Why ain't I with them! oh, misery! There, there drops a Mahometan! and now another—and another! Good, another one! Bravo, Lord Alonzo!—Ha! look at them run like a flock of rabbits. But, what! O God! is it possible? No; it cannot be!

DON VASCO. (*Rising.*) What! What do you see? Do our soldiers flee?

PEDRILLO. No, no! not that! It is not that!

DON VASCO. Away, and let me see myself.

PEDRILLO. No, no! Lord Vasco; stay there, I beg you! Too soon you will know it all!

(*Enter* TARIK, PEDRO, FABRICIO, *Spaniards and Mahometans.* ALONZO *is borne in on the arms of the Spanish soldiers.*)

DON VASCO. My son! my son! is he hurt?

TARIK. Your son! is he hurt? My sword is broken in his wounded side. For the first time my hand failed me; I wished to pierce his heart.

DON VASCO. Sir cavalier, add not insult to misery.

TARIK. (*To* ALONZO.) 'Tis thus, then, most worthy son, you keep your word! Was I wrong to doubt your sincerity?

DON VASCO. Spaniards, away with him!

ALONZO. Hold, father! let him upbraid me with my infidelity. I gave you my allegiance, Tarik, in betraying my God. In returning to Him, could I keep it? Spaniards, approach. Tarik, hear me. Father, let me lay my aching

head on your kind bosom. I have been very criminal; you
all have seen me wear the cursed livery of Mahomet—and
yet, within the depths of my heart I was always a Christian!
Ambition blinded me; vengeance and hate urged me on. But
God has guarded me—has recalled me to Himself. I offer
Him the humble sacrifice of my life. Father, bless me; your
son dies a Christian! Soldiers, be always faithful to your
God; obey your king; love your country; and, sometimes,
when in the evening before our Holy Mother's shrine, do not
forget to think of and pray for me. Come nearer, good
Pedro. (*To Vasco.*) Lord, *he* was my father——when all
the others shrank from me. Farewell, my tongue already
grows thick in death. Farewell! father; farewell! I am going to the feet of Jesus, to pray for you—to pray for you,
my good and noble father! (*Dies.*)

PEDRO. Happy Fernando, may the angels bear thy soul
'mid heavenly harmony to thy eternal home!

DON VASCO. Son of Gomez, thy death is worthy of thy
name; thou hast died fighting for thy God!

TARIK. It was I who snatched your tender lamb from
your care,—why, then, longer delay my punishment?

DON VASCO. What do you await from me?

TARIK. Death!

DON VASCO. Death! thy god can give that; as for mine,
He pardons.

TARIK. Even though I have killed your son!

DON VASCO. My son! Begone, Tarik; leave me to weep
over my boy. You are my prisoner, but fear not for life, it
is not mine; it belongs to God.

TABLEAU.

END.

THE MALEDICTION.

The following is the last Scene of the Third Act remodelled for the St. Cecilians, of the University of Notre Dame, Ind., on their *debut* in this play—in 1875.

(*Enter* TARIK, *running.*)

DON VASCO. My son, my son! is he hurt?

TARIK. Your son: is he hurt! My sword pierced his side. For the first time my hand failed me; I wished to pierce his heart.

DON VASCO. Sir cavalier, add not insult to injury.

TARIK. It is thus, then, that your most worthy son kept his word! Was I wrong to doubt his sincerity?

DON VASCO. Pedrillo, away with him!

PEDRILLO. (*Approaching* TARIK.) You, mister, shut up your bill and smother your tongue; hey! will you?

TARIK. (*Menacing* PEDRILLO. Away!

PEDRILLO. (*Going backwards.*) Oh! please, Mr. Mahometan, be careful in your movements; you might hurt somebody. (*Aside.*) What a face! his nose is like a frog's tail; his lips are big enough to play a cattle-drum. Ah, blockhead! stubborn fool! senseless coward! if I catch hold of you, I'll make you undergo a change of all colors.

TARIK. What say you, dog?

PEDRILLO. (*Aside.*) Dog! dog! that's all he can say. (*To* TARIK.) Oh! I say—in that—way—that—I say nothing.

(*Enter* PEDRO, *alarmed.*)

PEDRO. Lord, Lord Don Vasco! your son is fallen in the battle. (*Perceiving* TARIK.) Ho! here, here is the tyrant; here is the murderer of Don Alonzo! What! shall no one avenge the atrocity of the crime? He has snatched Alonzo from his religion; from his family; from his sacred duties; and now he has drenched his sword in his blood! Ho! here is the cause of the malediction! Who shall be the avenger? Pedrillo, my son, show thy courage; fear no longer for thy life, for honor shall compensate for it. Avenge the death of Don Alonzo.

PEDRILLO. O yes, father, surely I will; my sword is new, but the better for it. I'll shorten the ears of that monster.

TARIK. You coward!

PEDRILLO. Yes, of course, I am a coward: dog; senseless, and anything you wish. (*He pulls out his sword, and tries to strike* TARIK *on the head; but the blow being prevented, the fencing commences. After a certain length of time* TARIK *falls beneath the sword of* PEDRILLO.)

DON V. and PEDRO. Heaven!

(*Enter* FABRICIO, SPANIARDS, *and* MAHOMETANS—ALONZO *is borne in on the arms of the* SPANISH SOLDIERS.)

DON VASCO. My son, my son yet living!

DON ALONZO. Oh, father! let me lay my aching head upon your kind bosom. I have been very criminal; you all have seen me wearing the cursed livery of Mahomet—and yet, within the depths of my heart I was always a Christian! Ambition blinded me; vengeance and hate urged me on. But God has guarded me—has recalled me to Himself. I offer Him the humble sacrifice of my life. Oh, father! Tarik is your prisoner, but I beg of you to preserve his life— I forgive him.

DON VASCO. My dear Alonzo, Tarik is no longer living: the God of Justice has already judged him. Here lies his body.

ALONZO. Heaven! Father, bless me. Your son dies; but he rather joyful, he dies a Christian. Soldiers, be always faithful to your God; obey your king; love your country; and, sometimes, when before our Holy Mother's shrine, do not forget to think and pray for me. Good Pedro, approach. (*To* DON VASCO.) My lord, he was my father—when all the world repulsed me——Farewell, my tongue already grows thick in death. Farewell! father: farewell! I am going to the feet of Jesus, to pray for you—for you, my good—and—noble father! (*Dies.*)

PEDRO. Happy Fernando, may the angels bear thy soul 'mid heavenly harmony to thy eternal home!

(*Illumination—Music from the Orchestra—Tableau.*)

CURTAIN.

END.

ERRATA.

In "Mendoza's" song, page 10, the reader will change as follows:

The 6th line of 1st stanza should read:

> Let our nation's war-cry ring
> Freedom, etc.

Second and third lines in 2d stanza:

> My mother's dying form they trod,
> Sightless eyes she raised and smiled.

PROLOGUE.

The downward path of folly leads
To reckless thoughts, to 'vengeful deeds.
And when the will has been given o'er
To evil counsel, life no more
Presents glad views of hope and light;
For all things bear the deadly blight
That falls on souls, from truth perverted,
And Nature's self is disconcerted.

In the *dénouement* of our play
This axiom fixed we shall portray.

A Christian Noble, lured by guile,
Becomes a Renegado vile:
Ambition's specious, boastful din,
Has drowned the voice of Faith within:
It drags him to the fatal brink;
His conscience seared, he *will not think*:—

Renounces father, Country, God:—
Don Lopez and the Turks applaud:
But though the flatteries of the foe
Like waters of the Xenil flow,
Poor Don Alonzo finds no rest,
For latent faith stirs in his breast:
And when vicissitude of war
Brings his wronged father from afar,
And faithful Vasco meets his son,
Who strives that father's gaze to shun.
How cold Ambition turns the scale!
How the Apostate's glories pale!

The battle he has won has brought
That Sire whose love was set at nought,—
Brought him a prisoner, doomed to die,
Unless he will his faith deny.

The turbaned renegado prince
Before such presence well may wince;
What now his empty "pride of place"
Before this climax of disgrace?
What profit in that Moslem crown
That calls God's malediction down?
We will not here anticipate
The plot, but will the scenes await,
Which show when son to sire was known
The youth's proud intellect was thrown

From its mad height. Of reason 'reft,
What had his Turkish kingdom left?
The false heart, drawn from bad to worse,
Writhes 'neath a Christian father's curse.

Time flies: repentance comes at length,
And reparation, with the strength
Of Reason to her throne restored,
Balm on his sin-crushed heart is poured.
A Christian, once again, he fell
At last (O joy the tale to tell!)
In contest for the Eternal truth,
Which nurtured him in guileless youth.
While Tarik died, as brutes expire,
Than theirs his hopes knew nothing higher.
But the repentant Spaniard rose
Victorious o'er his sensual foes;
For, dying in the cause of Heaven,
His sinful weakness was forgiven.

Let great Don Vasco's steadfast zeal
To every youthful heart appeal,
That all may, free from folly's fiction,
Shun Don Alonzo's Malediction.

EPILOGUE.

"A pendulum betwixt a smile and tear"
Man has been called, and so it must appear
In this our Drama.
                    That amusing fellow,
So brave in safety, named by us Pedrillo,
May represent a very numerous class,
Who let the pith of any moral pass:
Yet, all the laughter that he has excited
Has harmed no one: in truth, it was invited:
But it would prove a subject of regret
If "yellow satin" and the "red rosette,"
The glittering jewel, and the waving plume
Should rob our Drama of its sweet perfume.
That is to say, should laughter and gold lace
Divert our thoughts from action of God's grace,
Which made Don Vasco ready to lay down
His noble life to win the martyr's crown.

This is the thought; the main and clear intention,
For which, kind friends, we claim your condescension
His firmness forms the model high of youth;
The mark of merit is to stand by truth
Amid disasters, hatred and contempt:
He who does this from blame must be exempt.
His mind of sterling metal has been made,
Justice by him will never be betrayed.
Beneath Don Vasco's banner, face and flank,
May every St. Cecilian proudly rank;
Yet, in Alonzo, let the false heart see
What course shall set the slavish spirit free.
Enough of precept!
                    Thank your lenient smile
On our attempt your evening to beguile:
Here, oft again each kindly face to view
We hope, good friends; meanwhile, we say adieu!

NEW BOOKS.

JOSEPH HAYDN.—THE STORY OF HIS LIFE, translated from the German of Franz Von Seeburg by the Rev. J. M Toohey, C. S. C., Vice-President of the University of Notre Dame Ind 350 pp. Price. · · · · $1.50

THE AMERICAN ELOCUTIONIST AND DRAMATIC READER, for the Use of Colleges, Academies, and Schools. Contains the celebrated Drama, "The Recognition." 468 pp. Price, $1.50.

THE HOUSEHOLD LIBRARY OF CATHOLIC POETS, from Chaucer to the Present Day. The only work of its kind in the Language. Subscription Edition (with an admirable portrait of Chaucer). Price, $5.00; Cheap Edition, · $2.00

THE SCHOLASTIC ANNUAL for 1884 Ninth year. Price, 25c.

NEW PLAYS.

FOR MALE CHARACTERS ONLY.

THE MALEDICTION. A Drama in Three Acts. Translated and adapted from the French. Price, · · · 50c.

IF I WERE A KING. A Drama in Four Acts. Price, 50c.

LE BOURGEOIS GENTILHOMME; OR THE UPSTART. A Comedy in Three Acts, adapted from the French of Moliere. Price, · · · · · · · · · 25c.

ROGUERIES OF SCAPIN. A Comedy. Translated from the French. Price, · · · · · · · 25c.

Other dramas in course of preparation.

Any of the above publications sent free of postage on receipt of retail Price. A liberal discount to dealers and those purchasing in quantities.

Address, **J. A. LYONS,**
NOTRE DAME, IND.